zane

the bad boys of saddle creek
book one

Kat Baxter

zane

A FRIENDS WITH BENEFITS/CURVY *Girl Romance*

Emmy

I am a walking nerdy girl cliche. Smart? Check! On the spectrum? Check! Awkward? Check! Virgin? Check! The only nerdy-girl box I don't check is "friendless." That's because I have the coolest best friend ever—Zane. Everyone in town thinks Zane is just a hot, bad boy inkslinger, but I know better. With me, he's kind, sensitive and thoughtful. I know he doesn't see me as anything more than a friend, but when I decide it's time to lose my virginity so I can finally date and find love, he's the only man I can imagine asking for help.

Zane

Emmy thinks we're just friends, but I know better. I've been in love with her for damn near half my life. Until now, I could be satisfied being just her best friend. But now that I know she's ready for a physical relationship with a man, all bets are off. She wants help losing her virginity so she'll be comfortable dating some super geek she works with? Fine. I will take her V-card, but I plan on ruining her for other men.

Zane

Kat Baxter

Copyright 2023 by Kat Baxter

This novel is a work of fiction. Names, characters, places and incidents are either the product of the author's imagination or have been used fictitiously and are not to be construed as real. Any resemblance to persons, living or dead, actual events, locales or organizations is entirely coincidental.

All Rights Reserved.

No part of this book may be reproduced or transmitted in any form, or by any electronic or mechanical means, including photocopying, recording, or by an information storage and retrieval system, without the express written permission of the author or publisher, except where permitted by law.

Edited by: Emily Beierle-McKaskle

Copyeditor: BookReadingJenn

Book cover: Cormar Covers

With regard to digital publication, be advised that any alteration of font size or spacing by the reader could change the author's original format.

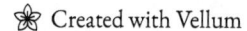

❦ Created with Vellum

chapter
one

Emmaline

Once a week, I have lunch with the most handsome man in town.

I'm sure that seems like an exaggeration, since I'm an awkward, weirdo, nerdy girl who makes everyone uncomfortable. But it's the honest truth.

I'm not even talking about eating lunch at home with my cat, who is admittedly a very handsome boy. I eat most of my meals at home alone, with Miles Standoffish, said cat, or with Miles and my sister, Lily. Generally speaking, I don't like eating in public; I never seem to get the eating to talking ratio right. I never know when it's the right time to talk and when it's the right time to listen. And that's true even when there isn't food involved.

Besides, other people's mouths are gross and I don't like hearing people chew. Which, I know, seems more about other people eating, but it still makes me uncomfortable. Because what if other people feel that way about me and my mouth? And don't even get me started with the noises in restaurants.

My point is, generally speaking, it's better for me to just eat at home with Miles.

But once a week, I make an exception and eat lunch with my best friend, Zane, who just happens to also be the most handsome man in town.

Today, we're at the diner, which is where we normally eat. I'm watching him from across the table while he tells me a story about the most recent tattoo he gave to one of the old ladies in the town's "blue-haired group." They're a collection of relatively hip old grannies who meddle in plenty of the lives in this town. When I say "relatively hip" I really mean, way cooler than I am, but also much older.

Thankfully, they mostly leave me alone. They probably think I'm a lost cause. Or they simply don't know what to do with me. Either way, I'm always grateful when people don't notice me.

Zane's blue eyes flare as he gets to the

climax of the story. "A scorpion. Can you believe that?"

I laugh until I snort trying to imagine Mrs. Hollis with a scorpion marring her weathered skin.

"It's pretty badass looking, too."

"If you did it, that's not surprising. All your ink is amazing."

His lips quirk up in a lopsided grin. The brow with the tiny ring in it slides up. "Thanks, Starfish. You're good for my ego."

With him looking at me like that, it makes me completely understand why women always go bonkers over him. He's a perfect specimen of male attractiveness.

I don't say that just because he's my best friend. It's an objective fact.

He has sculpted muscles without looking like he took drugs to get them. He has an easy, genuine grin that hints at dimples. Dimples you can't exactly see because he always has a perfect amount of scruff to hide them. The same dark shade as the hair on his head. The hair he keeps just this side of long, a bit too long to be considered tidy, but not long enough that he rocks a man bun. Combined with how bright and vivid his blue eyes are, he's shockingly handsome.

But I've known from the moment Zane and I first became friends that I was destined to be that and nothing more. So, while I can objectively see that he is hot, as my twin sister, Lily, would say, I don't look at him that way.

The truth is, I don't look at any man that way. It's just not something I'm comfortable thinking about. But especially not Zane. I couldn't. Else I'd be setting myself up for a heartbreak that makes no sense.

Just then, Ruthie stops by the table with our slices of pie. Zane and I have a late lunch here every Wednesday because, one, it is one of the days I go into the actual office instead of working from home. And two, Wednesdays Ruthie makes homemade chocolate custard pie, and it is my very favorite thing to put in my mouth.

"Here you go, you two," Ruthie says, setting the plates down.

After she walks away, Zane takes a sip of his coffee and I take a bite of my pie. I close my eyes as the smooth chocolate custard slides across my tongue. I moan. There is nothing in the world as good as Ruthie's chocolate custard pie. I'll go to my grave believing that.

"I don't think anyone in the world enjoys any food more than you enjoy that pie," Zane says. He takes a bite and nods. "It is damn tasty though."

"No, that is a completely inaccurate description of this decadent dessert. It is utterly perfect. The crust is buttery and flakey. The custard is rich and chocolatey without being too sweet, and the texture is smooth and velvety without being slimy at all. Nothing tastes this good."

His tongue slips out and rolls against his bottom lip. "I think we'll have to agree to disagree about that, Starfish."

"What else is better?"

"Nothing you're ready to hear about."

I'm about to ask him to clarify that obscure answer when the bells of the diner door ring and in walks Daniel Clute.

I look down abruptly at my pie, trying to avoid him seeing me.

Zane turns around and sees the man standing at the counter. Then he whips around to face me again. "Did that fucker mess with you? Because you know I'll kick his ass if he did."

I snort. "That would not be a fair fight. I'm pretty sure I weigh more than Daniel." I whisper his name.

Dan sits at the counter waiting for a to-go order.

"Details, Starfish. Why are you acting weird? Who is that guy?"

I stare at Zane but say nothing.

"You know I won't let it go." He shifts in his seat as if he's about to stand. "Maybe I'll introduce myself. He looks like he's new in town."

I reach across the table and grab his hand. "Don't."

"Tell me who he is and why you're freaking out," Zane says.

"His name is Daniel and he works for J&D Funds, like I do." Zane is still watching me so carefully, even I can tell he's waiting for me to say more. That's one of the things I love about being with him. He's okay with the quiet, awkward moments, the slow pace it takes me to put my thoughts together and assemble them into order. "In fact, there is a lot about him that's like me."

"Okay," Zane stretches out the word.

"We have a lot in common. He's on the spectrum and he's a programmer." Zane quirks an eyebrow, and I roll my eyes. "Okay, arguably a lot of programmers are on the spectrum. But he has noise issues and doesn't like sushi." I hold a finger up. "And he thinks bananas are too squishy, just like I do. And I bet if I asked, he'd think mouths are gross, too." I nod for emphasis.

"If you know him, why are you trying to avoid him seeing you?" Zane asks.

Okay, so clearly, I didn't explain that as

well as I thought I did. Or maybe it's just that Zane is so used to all of my idiosyncrasies that he doesn't realize how rare it is to meet anyone else you think you can get along with. So, I mentally backtrack and try to explain it again. "You know how I've always said that I'll be single forever because I'm just not built for coupledom?"

He nods slowly, his jaw ticking.

"Since Daniel," I whisper his name again, "and I are so similar, it makes me think that perhaps I was too hasty in my decision about single life. I mean with the right person, someone who knows what to expect from me and what I'm incapable of, it might work."

"I've been telling you that for years," he says, his voice low.

"I know." Zane has always said that, because that's the kind of wonderful, supportive friend he is. "But some things I guess I have to figure out on my own."

"So, what, you're like hot for that guy?"

"I don't get hot for guys, you know that." I've nearly finished my pie despite feeling apprehensive about Daniel being in the diner. Thankfully he still hasn't seen me. Zane hasn't even touched his pie. One of his hands grips his coffee mug so tightly, his knuckles have whitened.

He is so protective of me. It is truly the

sweetest. I reach across the table again and put my hand on his arm. "I promise he hasn't done anything to me. In fact, we've only had like, two conversations."

"Yet, you're ready to give it all up to him?" Zane snaps.

I stare at him for a minute and then shrug. "Well, no. It just seems like if I'm going to be with anyone, he's the type of person I could be with."

Zane's gaze narrows. Something about the way he's looking at me makes me uncomfortable. It's the same kind of discomfort I feel when I realize I've said or done something awkward, but I only realize it after the fact.

Which is how I often feel around other people. I know when I've done the wrong thing, but there's this delay. I only realize it after the fact, so I never know what exactly I said or did wrong.

Normally, I'm so comfortable around Zane, I don't ever feel like this.

I drop my gaze to what's left of my pie and stab at it listlessly with my fork. "I shouldn't have said anything."

After a moment, he blows out a breath. "No. It's fine."

"But I annoyed you."

"You surprised me. That's all. I thought

if you—" He cuts himself off and blows out another breath. "I just don't want you to rush into anything. Just because you have things in common with him, that doesn't mean you'll be compatible."

I frown, considering his words. "But we are compatible. Because we have a lot in common."

His lips tilt up in a hint of a smile. It's funny how I don't notice when other people barely smile, but I do when it's Zane.

"I don't mean compatible personalities. I mean physically." He clears his throat. "Sexually."

"Oh." I sit back, giving my pie another stab. "Does that matter?"

He chuckles. "Yeah. Quite a lot. Especially since you don't have a lot of experience."

And that's something I hadn't even considered. This is why I need Zane in my life. He sees things from a totally different perspective than me. Before I try anything new, I always do a considerable amount of research and studying.

That should apply here, especially since Daniel is the first person I've ever met who I could imagine having a relationship with.

"No, you're right. I don't want to mess this up. I might not ever meet someone as perfect for me again." Zane makes a weird throat noise and I look up at him. "Are you choking?"

"What? No."

"Oh, you made a weird noise. That's all." I eat another bite of pie, thinking over the idea.

If Daniel is my only shot at coupledom—and my lack of potential mates before now suggests he might be—then I need to approach the matter carefully. I can't rush things. I need to be emotionally and physically prepared to maximize my chances of success.

It's like when Mom used to quiz me with flashcards to help me learn how to recognize facial expressions. It was so dull, but she swore it would help me learn how to interact with neurotypical people. And I suppose it did. After all, here I am now, with a neurotypical best friend, eating pie in a restaurant with all these other people, and all their loud mouths.

And since Mom isn't here to help with this, I just need some other way to learn. I wonder if anyone makes physical intimacy flash cards?

Probably not.

I don't even know how I would Google that to find out.

Or maybe there are intimacy coaches? Because surely I'm not the only one who...

And that's when it hits me. Zane would be the perfect instructor.

"Can you one and done with just anyone?" I blurt.

"What the fuck does that mean?"

"I think you're right. I can't just jump into things with Daniel. I need someone to show me the ropes, as it were, sexually. The sexual ropes and you're the sexiest guy I know. Also, I trust you, which is a big deal. But if you can't one and done with just anyone, then it might not work?"

chapter **two**

Zane

I know, intellectually speaking, that I have zero reason to be so damn angry. It doesn't change the fact that I want to get up, cross to that doofus at the counter and rip his fucking head off.

That puny guy didn't even glance in Emmaline's direction since he walked in. Which is just a sign of what a dumbass he is, because she's always the first thing I look at in every room.

Clearly, he hadn't noticed her at all, or how fucking gorgeous she looks today. Her pale, whitish-blonde hair is in a side braid, across her shoulder—like Elsa. Fuck off, I know my animated princesses.

She's wearing one of her favorite t-shirts. The pink one with the cartoon cat that's not supposed to be a cat. Whatever. But the way her big tits make Hello Kitty's eyes look even bigger as the fabric stretches across her ample curves is damn mesmerizing.

She has a lot of Hello Kitty stuff. Once she told me that's what she feels like. Hello Kitty is a human on the inside, but she looks like a cat. She's different from everyone else in these overt and obvious ways, so sometimes people forget that she's a person on the inside.

I'm still trying to process everything she's said in the last fifteen minutes when she busts out with, "I mean, could you teach me how to do all the sex stuff?"

What is she even thinking?

All of sudden, she wants a physical relationship?

With that guy?

With *that* fucking guy?

Jesus. How am I supposed to even wrap my brain around this?

All I know is, I can't talk about this with her because it changes fucking everything. I feel like the foundations of my world are crumbling and there's no way I can sit here and just eat pie.

I pull some bills from my wallet and toss them on the table.

"I gotta go," I mutter. Then I do something I've never done before; I walk out on her.

My tattoo shop, the one I co-own with my older brother, Ian, isn't far. The diner is on the town square, and the shop is a block or so off the square, on the other side, so I walk. Rapidly. By the time I get there, my anger has reached a pinnacle. I walk in the door, then slam it behind me.

"God fucking dammit!" I bellow.

My brother and Harper, my sorta apprentice, look up from the small table we keep in the back for having quick meals.

"What flew up your ass?" Ian asks.

I just shoot him the finger because I don't want to talk about it.

Harper's brows furrow with concern.

Harper and I became close last year, when her guy, Johnny, had his head up his ass and was being a dumbass. Everyone knew they belonged together, but he was dragging his feet. Now, she's one of my best friends. "Uh-huh, you're not bottling this up, whatever it is. What happened?"

There's a buzz at the table. Ian holds up his phone. "Why is Emmaline texting to ask if you're okay?"

Fuck. If Emmaline is texting Ian, then I really fucking blew it.

"We just had a disagreement. It's not a big deal," I say.

My brother frowns. "Kind of a big deal. Y'all never fight."

What? Does he think I need him to tell me that?

Because I don't.

I know we never fight. Just like I know this problem is on me.

She never—not once in all our years of friendship—indicated she might want more from me. I'm the idiot who caught feelings. I'm the idiot who fell in love with my best friend.

And all this time, I told myself it was okay. That I could handle it. Because I knew she wasn't interested in anything physical. With anyone. I knew I was her person. I told myself that was enough.

But now? Now that she thinks this guy Daniel might be the guy for her?

Fuck that noise.

I stop pacing long enough to notice that Harper and Ian are staring at me.

"Doesn't anyone work in this damn place anymore? Why don't you have an appointment?"

"Little brother," Ian stands, "if you need to take the rest of the day off to cool your ass down, do it. Harper and I can handle things here. But don't be fucking biting my head off for asking a simple question." Then he gives me a hard look, before walking out to the front of the shop, leaving me with Harper.

She digs in her purse and holds out a package of Twizzlers, my favorite candy.

"What's this?" I ask.

"Pretty self-explanatory, Z."

I roll my eyes. "Why?"

"I don't know, honestly. I saw them at the checkout this morning when I stopped by the store to grab coffee because my brute of a husband keeps trying to monitor my caffeine intake, and I got them for you. Maybe I just instinctively knew you'd need them."

I snatch them out of her hand, and tear open the package with my teeth. "Your husband is just trying to be protective of your babies; give him a break."

"I think I liked it better when y'all didn't like each other," she says. She pulls out a rope of licorice when I offer her one. "Whatever's going on between you and Emmaline, let me help. Because you know you helped me out with Johnny even though he was such a dick to you."

"He was only a dick because he thought I was sniffing around his woman. Made him step up and claim you, didn't it? I knew y'all belonged together and I was fucking tired of all your moping."

She rolls her eyes. "Whatever."

We chew in silence for a couple of minutes before Harper speaks again. "You and Emmy have been friends for a long time. It's a strange friendship, I'm not gonna lie; y'all don't seem like you'd fit, but somehow you do." She tips her head to the side, watching me while she chews. "You're in love with her, aren't you?"

I lift a shoulder in a shrug. "Doesn't matter."

"Explain or I'm calling your brother in here and telling him you're crying."

I chuckle because I can't help it. Harper usually makes me laugh. "You're mean when you're pregnant, you know that?"

"Exactly. Now spill."

I blow out a slow breath. "Yes, I'm in love with her." I've never actually admitted that out loud to anyone. Not even myself. "Have been for forever, though it took me long enough to figure that out. But I made peace with the fact that she's not interested in having a physical relationship a long time ago. So, I have her in my life in the way that she's available to me and I've made that be enough."

"Oh, Zane."

"No! Do not feel sorry for me." I fiddle with the piercing in my tongue, pressing it against my teeth. "But now she's found some nerd who she thinks she can be compatible with, and she wants me to teach her how to 'do the sex.'"

Harper laughs and puts a hand over her mouth. "Is that what she said?"

"More or less."

"She doesn't know how you feel?" Harper asks.

I shake my head.

"Okay, you need to think about who you're talking about," Harper says. "Emmy is coming to this from a purely logical, non-emotional perspective. She never expected to have an emotional love, let alone a physical one. Right?"

"Yes. She's said forever that she wasn't the coupling kind."

"Well, now she's found someone who's clearly nonthreatening to her, and she's beginning to think maybe she could have a physical relationship. But you're the one she trusts. You can make this work for you, Zane."

"How the hell am I supposed to do that? Fuck her and then send her out to screw that other guy? That'll ruin everything, including our friendship."

Harper slaps me upside the head. Lightly, but still.

"That is not what I was suggesting, dumbass."

I rub at my ear where she hit me. "Then what are you suggesting?"

"She wants you to teach her about sex, right? So, use that to your advantage. Instead of teaching her just about sex, teach about sex *and* love. Teach her she'll never be happy with any man but you. Remind her how compatible y'all are. You're already a couple, in many ways, she just hasn't seen that yet."

chapter
three

Emmaline

Once I receive a text from Ian assuring me that Zane is fine, I go home bewildered. The truth is we've never had so much as a disagreement. We're very different people, anyone can see that, but we don't argue, and we don't fight. We just hang out and have a good time.

Honestly, our friendship has never made much sense to me. Why would someone so hot and so cool and so, so, so different from me, want to hang out with me? I never understood it, but after a while, I stopped questioning it and just enjoyed it.

Because the truth is that Zane is... well—if you can have a soulmate who's a friend—then that's what Zane is. He's my friendmate. No, that doesn't sound right. Well, whatever you call it, that's him. He's my person, my ride or die.

But now he's clearly angry with me and I don't know what to do about it. Once I get home, I go to my office, turning on all of my monitors so I can do this right.

I type out the scenario, and then I search for options. I import all the potential outcomes for such a scenario, then I write a program. I need algorithms to try and narrow down the possibilities.

I can figure this out.

By the time my twin sister, Lily, comes home, she finds me huddled in my office chair. Wrapped in my weighted blanket, I stare bleary-eyed at the monitors

"What are you doing?" she asks.

"I'm researching something." My voice is sharp, there's really nothing I could do about it.

"Hey, hey, don't bite my hand off." She crosses to the loveseat at the other end of the room and flops down. "What's up? What happened?

I spin my office chair and look at her. Her eyes are so similar to mine, the same pale, icy blue. The blue sky of Texas, that's what our mom had always called it.

"Zane and I had a fight. I think."

"You think?"

I shrug. "I think that's what it was. I don't know. I was asking him questions. And then he got really mad. And he left and I don't know what happened." I explain about the program I'm writing and show her the monitors with the possible scenarios. "The problem is, I just don't have enough data to work with."

"What do you mean you don't have enough data?"

"I should have started years ago, when we first became friends. If I'd been tracking our interactions and his mood over time, I might have enough input for the algorithms, but as it is, I only have this one data point and that's simply not enough to draw a conclusion about why he's mad."

"Wait, you wrote a computer program to figure it out?" she asks.

"Yes, that seemed the most logical, expedited course of action."

My sister is the one who's supposed to understand me better than anyone, since we shared a womb and she's on the spectrum, too. Although in different ways. Anyways, she looks at me and she laughs. Like hysterically laughs. Wiping-tears-from-her-eyes laughing.

"Oh, Emmaline," she says. "You are so extra."

"What the hell does that mean? I'm different, I know. Special, if you want to call it that. You're special. Mom and Dad said we were both special."

She shakes her head. "No, no. Not special like that. I just mean like, wow." She waves in the general direction of my computer set up. "*That* is some serious special." She wipes her eyes again.

"Okay, I'm gonna need you to break it down because I don't know what you're saying. And I feel like you're speaking in code, *and* that you're making fun of me, and I don't know how to decipher your meaning."

"Here it is. If you want to know why Zane is pissed, you need to ask him. Not your computers. You can't write a computer program to figure out why your best friend is pissed off."

I stare at her for a minute because, oddly enough, that solution didn't even come to mind. I knew he was angry with me, so I hadn't contacted him at all.

Why hadn't I thought to just simply ask him? Probably because we've never had any disagreements. I'm in uncharted territory. And I didn't know how to wade through it without him at my side. Because normally he's who'd I go too if I had a disagreement with someone else.

So if he's the one who's angry with me, how am I supposed to navigate this?

"Why don't you tell me what happened? What were you asking him when he got angry?" Lily asks.

I relay the situation about how we had been at lunch at Ruthie's and how Daniel had come in. I explain how I thought Daniel and I would be compatible because he is quirky and strange and nerdy and smart and all of the things that I am. "I asked Zane if he would help me with some stuff to get me ready for a relationship."

Lily's eyes narrow. "You asked your super-hot best friend if he would teach you how to *be* with other guys?"

"Well, yeah, I mean, he's got loads of experience, if the rumors are to be believed. I mean, I don't think poorly of him about it. But, you know, I guess some people do. He's a bad boy."

Even the term feels like a shiver across my skin, and I don't know why. Because it's not like he's actually a bad boy. He's a good guy. The *best* guy. Sweet, thoughtful, funny, so funny. And he loves all of the goofy, strange, sci-fi anything I could throw at him. We've had more movie nights and more binging weekends, over some obscure show. And it is always the best. No one laughs at those things like he does. Like I do.

So, I don't understand why thinking of him as a "bad boy" should make me feel hot and like my skin is too tight.

I throw off the weighted blanket, because surely that's causing the problem. "I think I'm overheating," I say. "Silly Texas winter."

"It's below forty outside, so you can't be that warm," Lily says. "So I think I figured out what's wrong."

"Why Zane is mad?"

She nods.

"Excellent, then you can just tell me."

"Nope. You need to ask Zane yourself. Y'all need to have this conversation."

I frown. That was not the easiest solution.

"Also, I need you to look up that guy Daniel and show me a picture because I need to see this for myself."

"Okay." I quickly lean forward and type up the name of our company and search the employee database. His work ID pops up on the screen.

His square, metal glasses don't add any color to his pale face. And the sandy blond hair just kind of wisps in thin streaks over his forehead. I try to imagine it's a roguish look, but in truth there's nothing roguish about Daniel.

My sister—like she's on drugs or something—cackles like a maniac. "Oh my God, this is too good."

I watch her giggle uncontrollably, annoyed that I'm not in on the joke.

"Yep, you're gonna need to contact Zane immediately. And then you're gonna have to report back to me what he says. Because I'm enjoying this way too much."

chapter
four

Zane

I don't even know what the fuck to do with myself. I hate that Emmy and I are fighting. I've already gone for a run and used the punching bag Ian and I keep in our garage.

Then I relent and ink yet another starfish onto my skin. This one is hidden within my sci-fi sleeve on my left arm. There are already others buried in that whole scene so what's one more?

Goddamn, I am one pathetic motherfucker.

My phone buzzes and I lean over to grab it.

Emmy's name lights up the screen with a text alert. Then another.

> Emmy: I don't like this.
>
> Emmy: I don't know how to fight with you.
>
> Emmy: I don't know what I did wrong.

I'm a jackass. Of course she doesn't know what's going on. She has no idea how I feel about her or that I'm a jealous bastard.

> Me: We're fine. You did nothing wrong.
>
> Me: I was just being a moody asshole.

The three dots appear, then disappear, then appear again. But no text comes through. So I just tap the button to call her.

"Impatient much?" she asks when she answers.

I chuckle. "Starfish, I just wanted you to hear my voice and know that we're okay."

"Okay. I'm still sorry if I upset you in some way."

"Emmaline, stop obsessing."

She blows out a breath.

"I do have thoughts about your predicament."

"About me being a never-been-kissed virgin?" she asks. Her tone is so casual, as if she'd actually been talking about an old pair of shoes.

"Yeah. I think you need to back it up a few steps."

"What does that mean?"

"You don't need sex lessons," I grind out the words.

Then, I blow out a breath, struggling to get my temper under control, because she does not need me acting like a jealous asshole right now.

As soon as I feel slightly more in control, I remember Harper's suggestion.

Okay, I can do this. I know in my gut that Emmy is mine. That if she's really ready for a physical relationship, that it should be with me. Because I know I will treat her right. I just need to convince her of that.

"You don't need sex lessons," I repeat, and thank fuck my voice sounds more normal. "At least not right away. You need couple lessons. Dating lessons."

She groans. "But isn't dating the worst? Everyone is always complaining about it."

"Don't worry about anyone else. Here's what we're going to do. This Friday, I want you to get dressed up. Wear something that you're comfortable in, but something that makes you feel pretty. Then I'm going to come get you and take you on a date. We'll start there."

Her sharp intake of breath makes me nervous for what she's about to say. "So you will help me?"

"Of course. You're my starfish. I'll always be here for you."

We chat about random things for another fifteen minutes before we hang up. Now I've got to come up with the perfect date to show her that I can be the man in her life. She doesn't need to settle for someone whom she thinks matches her. We already know we're compatible.

I know we'll have chemistry, I'm not even worried about that. I'm so hot for my curvy Emmy that I know once we're together, we'll set the fucking world ablaze.

chapter **five**

Emmaline

I give up on my hair and pull it into a high ponytail. It sorta makes me look sophisticated. Or at the very least that I tried to do something different with it besides braiding it. My hair is pale blonde and weirdly wavy. Not curly, not straight, just kind of these messy waves like I don't know how to brush it. So I generally wear it pulled away from my face so it doesn't annoy me.

My makeup is light, just enough to accent my eyes. And I'm wearing a dress.

"Whoa, you look hot!" my sister practically screams from my bedroom doorway.

"Lily! What is wrong with you?"

"Sorry, I just got excited." She comes into my room and plops onto my bed. "Seriously, though, you look *muy caliente*."

"Thanks." I press my palm to my belly.

"Are you nervous?" she asks.

It's on my tongue to tell her no, but the hoard of bats flapping around in my stomach tell a different story. "Yeah, a little. Don't know why. It's not like Zane and I haven't gone out before. I mean it's just Zane!"

"True. Super, ridiculously hot and devilishly sexy Zane," Lily says.

"You need to stop reading historical romances for a while," I say with a chuckle. "No one says devilish anymore."

"Well, they should. There's something so appealing about those stern, grouchy gentlemen who seem all starchy but are really dirty, dirty boys."

I laugh, which helps soothe my nerves.

"Your boobs look awesome in that dress, by the way," my sister says, pointing at my reflection.

And... the nerves are back. I glance down at my cleavage on bold display. "I should change. Put on a t-shirt and yoga pants."

"He told you to dress nicely, right?"

"He told me to wear something comfy, that makes me feel pretty."

Lily smiles at me. "Do you feel pretty?"

I look in the mirror at the way the sweetheart neckline of the black dress hugs my boobs. My eyes are bright—probably because of the nerves. My hair actually looks kinda artful rather than just messy. I smile.

"Yeah, I guess I do," I say.

Ding-dong.

"Oh, he's here." Lily claps her hands. "Want me to get the door so you can make a grand entrance?"

"Yes, because I need to get my shoes, but if you play Sixpence None the Richer's *Kiss Me*, I'll shiv you with a straw."

She cackles and leaves me to head to the door.

I slip on my favorite pair of low-top Chucks. They're so not fancy, but they're me. And it's not like Zane is going to be all fancied up.

"Holy shit!" Lily yells.

I run out to see what she's shrieking about and there he stands. He's not wearing a suit, but he's wearing black slacks that simultaneously fit him perfectly and hug his thick thighs. A metal-gray buttoned-down shirt is tucked in at his lean waist.

His hair is freshly trimmed and he's shaved.

My mouth is dry and probably hanging open.

He holds up a small bouquet of daisies. They're my favorite but no one has ever given them to me.

"Why do you look like a banker?" I ask.

Lily smacks my arm.

Zane quirks that lopsided grin at me and this time because of his beardless face, I see those dimples.

"I look like a banker?"

"Well, you look like a super sexy banker or at least a high-end realtor."

Lily grabs the daisies. "I'll put these in water," she chirps then leaves the room.

"Starfish, you look beautiful," he says. His sapphire eyes roam all over my body.

"Thanks."

"You ready?" He motions to the door.

I blow out a breath. "I guess so."

"Relax, Starfish, it's just me." He holds his hand out to me and threads our fingers together.

"Bye, you two," Lily says. "I won't wait up."

"You're the worst," I tell her, but I'm still smiling.

He leads me to his car and opens the door for me. Once I'm seated and buckled, he shuts the door and goes around to his side.

"Where are we going?" I ask, the minute he sits.

"You'll see. I know you don't like surprises, and this isn't *really* a surprise. I just want to wait until we're there."

"Sorry I called you a banker," I blurt.

"You called me sexy, too. So you're forgiven."

"Well, that's always the case. Every girl in town thinks that."

He reaches over and squeezes my knee. "I don't care what other girls think."

His words along with that innocent touch spread through my body like a wave of warmth, leaving tingles in its wake. I have to remind myself that this is just a practice date. He's merely getting me used to how things go with couples.

He pulls his car into a spot in front of his shop, *The Needle Bards*. Then he comes around to get me, again threading our fingers together. Our hands fit perfectly, our palms nestled against one another, in a way that feels so natural I wonder why we haven't been holding hands for years.

On the whole, I'm not someone who cares much for physical affection. I'm not a hugger. I don't enjoy feeling closed off by someone forcing their body next to mine, even in a harmless friendly gesture. But holding Zane's hand—much like hugging him, which I've done on occasion—feels soothing.

He leads me past his shop though and heads to the door to *Madison's Mercantile*, the general store owned by Madison used-to-be-Crawford Burton. The store's namesake opens the front door. Sheriff Burton, her husband, stands behind her with a hand on her hip.

I'm completely baffled by what we're doing here, but I stay quiet lest I drive everyone bonkers with my incessant questions.

"Welcome," Madison says with a smile. She hands keys to Zane. "Just lock up when you're done. The stairs are in the back room."

"Thanks again," Zane says.

"Y'all have fun," Madison says and shoots me a wink.

The sheriff merely nods at us and they head out the front door. "Come on, Trouble, let's go get you fed." He pats his wife on the bottom and they walk off.

I turn back to Zane. "What are we doing here?" I ask because I can't hold back any longer.

He locks the front door, pockets the keys, then drags me to the back of the store. When we reach the staircase leading up, we climb them together.

Then he opens a door and leads me out

onto the rooftop. It's flat with a brick border that frames the entire old store. There are some plants scattered around and a couple of chairs, but the candlelight surrounding the table set up for two is what draws my attention.

"Zane," I whisper.

"Come on, Starfish. Our food is probably getting cold." He leads me forward with a firm hand settled against the small of my back. His pinky finger rests halfway on the rise of my bottom.

Again that shiver of warmth spreads through my body.

Once he's pushed my chair to the table and set a napkin in my lap, he goes and sits on his side.

The rich aroma of fried seafood hits my noise and I close my eyes and inhale.

Then he pulls the metal plate covers off and my meal is revealed.

"You got my favorite from Gator's?" I ask.

"Of course." He pulls the bottle that's been chilling in an ice bucket up. "Sparkling apple juice?" he asks.

I laugh and swipe at my spontaneous tears because this man—my beautiful best friend—has created the perfect date for me. He knows I don't drink. I don't care for the taste of alcohol or how it makes me feel. But I love sparkling juice.

"Yes, please."

He pours us each a glass, then motions to my plate. "Eat."

I dig into my fried shrimp and that first bite explodes across my tongue with flavor. No one fries shrimp like Mr. Guidry. "You thought of everything. It's so perfect." I look around at the night sky, the stars twinkling above us, because at night Saddle Creek is still small enough that you can see a lot of celestial sky.

"No low hum of murmurs from other customers. No other mouth noises." I smile at him and pop another shrimp in my mouth. "Thank you."

"My starfish deserves the very best. Plus, I wanted you all to myself."

"You truly do look very handsome, but why did you change your look? Pull out your eyebrow ring and shave your beard?"

He sets his fork down and looks up at me. "That man you work with is clean shaven and unpierced, isn't he?"

"Daniel?" I ask after a few minutes because I had forgotten the true reason for this date. Disappointment weighs on my shoulders. "Yes, he is."

Zane shrugs. "I obviously can't look just

like him, but I wanted to you get a more accurate experience. Maybe see me a little differently."

"I see." So I can better pretend he's Daniel? No one would ever confuse the two. Zane is broad shouldered and inked on most of the skin I've seen, except his face and part of his hands. Zane has a natural brooding expression that evaporates into the most adorable smiles when he finds something amusing. Zane has visible muscles cording his forearms and neck. Zane is pure masculinity wrapped up in a super sexy package, but inside him beats a pure heart that loves his friends unconditionally. I could never look at Zane and think of Daniel or vice versa.

We finish our meals while debating whether or not the most recent Star Trek iteration is just a slick repackage of Next Generation.

He pulls out his phone and taps on the screen and soft music starts to play. Then he's at my seat holding a hand out to me.

"Dance with me, Emmaline."

I open my mouth, then close it, choosing instead to put my hand in his. I can dance. Sorta.

He pulls me into his arms, close like a hug, but he's got one hand holding mine and the other is wrapped around my waist. From this close, I know he can feel the squishiness of my belly and the heavy press of my boobs.

But oh, wow, he smells good. Like the beginnings of a spring rain and freshly trimmed grass—after all the obnoxious Texas pollen has cleared the air.

I lay my head on his shoulder and let him lead me around the roof.

We dance through two songs before he pulls back a little. "I have pie," he says with a waggle of his brows.

"Pie?"

"Yes. Ruthie's chocolate custard pie. A whole one just for us."

"Oh my God, Zane Miller, I love you."

He laughs and we go back to the table for a slice of pie.

Everything about this date is perfect and clearly his plan is working because I'm feeling the physical things that women talk about in romance novels.

The excitement kind of nerves that bubble in your body, instead of tightening. The weird, heightened awareness of my own body. Like right now I'm very aware that my cleavage is on display, and my nipples have been tight pretty much all evening. It's not the weather. Despite it being wintertime, tonight has been unseasonably warm.

Not that Zane is looking because he's parking his car in front of my house. When he walks me to my front door, he once again holds my hand.

"I had a really good time tonight, Starfish," he says, giving me that lopsided grin.

"I did too. It was perfect."

"It's not quite perfect."

I'm about to ask him why, but he cups my cheek with one hand and pulls me flush to him with the other. Then his lips brush against mine. Gentle and sweet.

Then I lick my bottom lip and he takes the opportunity to slide his tongue against my lips as well. I moan at the sensation.

I tentatively sweep my tongue into his mouth and he releases a low growl in his throat. I'd always thought the notion of French kissing sounded gross and unnecessary. But I have completely changed my mind. Kissing Zane is a revelation.

He pulls away before I'm ready, and smiles at me. He kisses my forehead, then squeezes my hand. "Goodnight, Emmy." Then he walks back to his car, leaving me confused and more than a little turned on.

. . .

I close the house door behind me and lean against it, eyes shut.

"Emmy, you okay?"

My sister's voice startles me. "Yeah. I think so." I walk into the kitchen and grab a glass of water, downing it in one go.

"Whoa," Lily says. "You sure? You don't seem okay?"

I set down the glass. "Zane kissed me."

She pumps her fist. "Yes! Finally!"

"What do you mean finally?" I ask.

"Tell me you haven't been dreaming of that since y'all met!"

"Honestly? I don't think I have. I've always suspected I wouldn't like kissing. You know how I feel about other people's mouths." I shudder just thinking about it. "But kissing Zane was nice. Better than nice."

"I imagine so. Isn't his tongue pierced?" Lily asks.

I frown. "Yes, but I don't think I noticed that."

She grabs my hand and pulls me to our sofa and we sit. "Talk to me, Em, what are you thinking?"

"I don't know. I started this whole thing because I found a guy at work who seems like the most compatible person for me if I was going to be in a relationship. But honestly, I can't imagine letting Daniel hold my hand.

Or dancing with him." I shake my head. "I especially don't think I want to kiss him. He's a mouth breather."

Lily's brows go up. "Isn't that a deal breaker for you?"

"I don't know. I feel like maybe I've been too picky. Daniel is my speed. We are a lot alike."

"You have a lot in common with Zane, too," Lily says. "You can't forget that."

I smile. "He's my very favorite person in the world besides you. But we're not like that. He's only doing this to get me comfortable with other people."

"You sure about that?"

"Oh yes. I mean he kissed the hell out of me, then just turned around and left me on the porch. So casual, so cool. Meanwhile I was standing there like a puddle of goo."

My sister squeezes my hand.

"I've never been so aware of my body as I was tonight." I shake my head and stand. "I'm just going to go to bed and maybe my subconscious will have a solution for me in the morning. But I think the best option is to call off this fake dating, couple training thing with Zane."

"Don't be too hasty."

"I don't want to screw up my best relationship just because I had a wild hair idea about maybe having a boyfriend."

I go through my bedtime routine, then crawl between my cool sheets. Miles jumps up on the mattress and curls into my side. His little paws make biscuits on the covers, and I scratch him behind the ears.

"If only life were as simple for me as it is for you, sweet boy."

He looks up at me with sleepy green eyes and blinks slowly.

My body is still humming with remnants of arousal from Zane's kiss. The way he growled. The way he held my face and my body at the same time. The way he tasted, like my favorite pie, sweet and sinful.

I cannot afford to have feelings like this about my best friend. I should never have suggested to him he be the one to teach me these things. Thank goodness he had enough sense to start with a date rather than us jumping into bed. I'd be a complete goner.

The fact that he was able to simply walk away after the kiss we shared, so casual and unaffected, says everything. Granted it was my first kiss, but still.

It is for the best—both for my heart and the preservation of our friendship—that we stick to just being friends.

chapter
six

Zane

It's late and I'm at the shop alone. Ian has flown to Vegas for the first of a couple of trips to ink an old buddy of his who lives out there. I came here after our date, because I have too much energy to go home and too many thoughts burning through my brain to be out in public. So, I've been giving the shop a thorough cleaning, working like the health inspector is coming tomorrow, in hopes that I'll eventually hit a wall of exhaustion. I finish disinfecting my station when I hear a knock at the back door.

I fling it open ready to give Harper some shit about forgetting her key, but it's Emmaline standing there.

I swallow hard because—fuck—she looks

good. And now, after all these years, I know what she tastes like.

"Hey, Starfish," I say.

She doesn't say anything. She just pushes past me into the shop.

I close the door behind her and then turn to find her spinning her thumb ring.

"You want to sit down?" I ask.

She shakes her head.

Something is clearly bothering her, but if I rush her, it will just make things worse. "Okay if I sit?" I ask.

She stops pacing for a moment to look at me. "Yes."

I sit at the small round table in our back room.

"I'm sorry I put you in an awkward position," she says.

I wait for her to further explain. Emmy uses language efficiently, so I know she's simply organizing her thoughts to say what she needs to say in the most straightforward way.

"I really appreciate last night and everything you did. But it's obvious that you don't find me physically attractive enough. I don't want you to have to fake things with me." She looks over at me. "The sex things. There's no reason to put you in a position where you need to force yourself to touch me. I respect you too much as a friend to make you do something you clearly don't want to do."

I force myself to not have a physical reaction, but damn it's hard. Because it feels like she slapped me. "You're misinterpreting. That is not what's going on."

She shakes her head. "Zane, I'm serious. I'm inexperienced, but I think I can recognize when someone is coddling me."

I stand up because now my body is flooded with restless energy. I want to grab her and show her how much I want to touch her. Touch her fucking everywhere.

"Starfish, please just trust me when I say, the very opposite is true. I want you more than you can possibly know."

Her brow furrows as she stares at me, confusion etched in her every feature. Then she shakes her head. "You're so sweet to me. All the time and I love that about you. Truly. But right now I need brutal honesty."

I release a humorless laugh. "You want some honesty?"

"Yes," she says.

She wants honesty? Fine. But she's not listening to me. And I'm done talking anyway.

I pull off my t-shirt, exposing my torso, all my ink and my pierced nipples. I unfasten my black leather belt, the metal from the buckle clanging. All the while I walk towards her. I undo my jeans button, then lower my zipper. I don't look at her face, not yet, I just let myself stare at her gorgeous curves. Let myself look at her with all the heat and lust I feel. She has to see it in my face.

By the time I reach her, she's backed herself up against the small cabinet and sink.

"Zane, what are you doing?" she asks, her tone breathy.

I glance up at her face, but she's staring at my body. Her pupils are wide and she licks her bottom lip.

"I'm showing you since you don't seem to believe my words," I say.

"Showing me what?" Finally, her eyes flick to mine.

"You have it all wrong, Emmaline Granger. I didn't walk away from you last night because I don't want you." I reach into my boxers and pull out my hard cock. Yeah, it's pierced too. "I had to walk away from you because I want you so fucking much, I'm terrified of scaring you off."

"You liked kissing me?" she asks. She glances at my face, but then her gaze is back, locked on my exposed dick.

"So much. Do you want to know what I had to do as soon as I got home?" I drag my fist up my erection, then back down. "I barely made it into my bedroom before I had my cock out and I was jerking it to the memory of your sweet mouth."

She sucks in a breath. "I want to watch you."

Honestly, I have no idea how I expected her to respond when I pulled out my dick. Still, her reaction shocks me.

"Right now? You want me to fuck my hand and show you what you do to me?"

"Yes," she whispers.

Her nipples are hard. I can see them poking against her black t-shirt. It has a cartoon sloth on it holding a gaming controller and in big letters it says, "Pew. Pew."

It's dorky and silly and so perfectly Emmaline. I don't know how my girl can be so sexy dressed in a simple t-shirt, but she is.

I want to press against her. Grab her hand and wrap it around my dick. I want to kiss her again, slide my tongue to hers and hear those sweet little whimpers she made in the back of her throat. But I need her to feel like she's in control.

Because she is the one in control here. Whatever she wants, however much she wants, I'm here for it. I'm here for her.

I lower my boxers enough so my entire junk is revealed to her.

"You're pierced there, too," she says, her voice sounding breathless in a way I've never heard before.

"My frenum," I explain. "It's one of the most sensitive spots on a penis and rubs a woman in just the right spot during sex."

She reaches out like she wants to touch the barbell, but then pulls her hand back. "Did it hurt?"

"When I had it done? Yeah. But it feels good now." I show her by rubbing a finger across the metal bar, then tug on it. I groan.

"Show me, Zane. Show me what you had to do," she says.

I brace me feet apart, my boots squeaking on the linoleum floor. Then I stare at my girl and shuttle my hand up and down my cock.

"You have no idea how many times I've had to do this after I've spent time with you."

"But I thought the kiss—"

"The kiss was fucking hot. So damn perfect. But it's you that turns me on, Starfish."

I move my hand faster, squeezing my shaft tight.

Emmy shifts her feet, as if trying to get more comfortable.

"Fuck, I bet your panties are soaked right now. Aren't they?"

She swallows and looks up at my face briefly. Her head nods in agreement.

"I'm getting close, Emmy. Goddamn it." I groan as my balls tighten and I come. Ropes of my release hit the floor and my stomach.

When it finally ends, I look up at her to see her watching me with wide eyes and lips parted. Her tongue slips out to moisten her lips and it's the hottest thing I've ever seen.

I want to reach for her, but instead I reach for the paper towels.

Emmy's hand stills my reach. "Wait." She comes closer and extends one fingertip. She swipes through the cum decorating my stomach, then brings her sample to her nose and inhales. "Salty and clean smelling."

Then she puts that finger close to her mouth.

"The texture might bother you," I say. Unsexy, but my girl is sensitive to certain textures.

"I still want to taste it." Then she slides that fingertip into her mouth and moans.

I was wrong before. This is the sexiest thing I've ever seen.

"Starfish," I say.

Then her palm presses to my stomach and smears my release between her hand and my abs.

"I like it," she whispers. Her hand slides down, exploring lower on my body.

My dick stirs. I grab her wrist and still her movement.

"You need to leave right now, or I won't be able to control myself." I squeeze my eyes closed. "I just came and you're making me hard again."

"I'm not afraid of you, Zane," she says.

"What does that mean?"

"That you're not going to scare me away." Then she kisses me.

chapter
seven

Emmaline

He growls into my mouth, reaches down, and cups my bottom. There's a squeeze and then he lifts me. Instinctively I wrap my legs around his waist. His hardening cock is trapped between our bodies and I'm so thankful I'm wearing yoga pants. That hard ridge of his dick presses to my cotton-covered core and I rock myself against him.

His lips leave my mouth to trail hot licks and nibbles down my throat.

"Will you take me home with you? I know your brother is out of town," I say.

He leans back a little, still holding me wrapped around him as if I were a tiny, petite thing instead of a plus-size woman with untouched curves.

That pierced brow rises. "You want me to take you back to my place?"

"Yes. I want to get naked and do all the things." I shake my head. "Okay, maybe not all the things; I don't think I'll ever want to do butt stuff."

He tips his head back and laughs. The motion rocks his erection against me and I squirm to try to get some relief.

"Please, Zane."

"I want that more than anything," he says. He lowers my feet so I slide down his body, then he grabs his shirt. He doesn't bother refastening his jeans, instead he just leaves the fly open.

Since he and Ian don't live too far from their shop, thankfully, the drive is quick. Especially since Zane's big hand is pressed to my core. He periodically strokes his fingers against my needy flesh. By the time he pulls my door open, my panties, and probably my yoga pants too, are soaked and I'm on the verge of an orgasm.

He grabs my hand and pulls me into the house and then straight into his bedroom.

"Starfish, you better tell me now if you don't want to do this, because I have very little blood flow to my brain at the moment."

I take his hand and shove it down the

front of my pants and panties. His thick fingers immediately sink between my wet folds.

"Fuck, Emmy, you're soaked." He gives me a heated kiss, then falls to his knees. Methodically, he removes my Chucks, then socks, then pulls off my yoga pants and underwear all in one motion.

I lean my head on the wall behind me.

He skims his hands up my legs, then leans forward and presses his forehead to my belly.

"You have no idea how long I've wanted to taste you," he says, his words edged with a growl.

His thumb swipes though my wetness.

"Zane," I say with a shiver.

He lifts one of my legs and places it over his shoulder. "That's it, Starfish, spread that pussy open for me. I need to fuck you with my tongue. Have you come all over my face."

His dirty words heat my cheeks. It's not off-putting, though. Quite the contrary. I seem to get wetter with every filthy thought he expresses.

The first brush of his tongue is exquisite. He licks all around my labia, as if he's cleaning up all my arousal. Then he plunges that tongue into my channel.

"Zane!"

True to his word, he fucks me with his

tongue. It only takes three thrusts before I'm rocking myself against his face. I thread my fingers through his hair.

I whimper and he chuckles against my sensitive flesh. Then his tongue retreats and is replaced by one of his thick fingers. His other hand squeezes my bottom.

"I was right, you know. You're fucking delicious."

His words settle into my pleasure-soaked brain. "What were you right about?"

"That there was something better than Ruthie's chocolate custard pie. I'm going to call it my Starfish pie."

I laugh because only Zane would say something like that. Think something like that.

He swirls his tongue around my clit, the little bead going rigid. Then there's another finger inside me. He moves them against my front vaginal wall and it's like the first time the Millennium Falcon goes into warp speed. Everything narrows to that one point.

"Zane, oh wow…"

He groans against me again, the vibrations enhancing my pleasure. And he keeps going. He's relentless in chasing my climax. My body is tight like one of those balls made of rubber bands. Any minute it's going to snap.

When it does, my world goes black and then technicolor explodes around me. Every pulse of ecstasy is a different color. I shudder against him as he licks me through every wave.

Then he sits back on his feet, wipes his chin on the shoulder of his shirt and stares up at me.

"Goddamn that was spectacular."

My body is boneless, but I can see the clear outline of his erection through his boxers. I hold a hand out to him and "help" him to his feet.

With him standing in front of me, I pull off my t-shirt and unhook my bra. I want him to see all of me. Every pale strip of skin.

chapter
eight

Zane

With the taste of her orgasm still fresh in my mouth, I pull her over to the bed. She's completely bare to me now and I want to touch her everywhere.

I take off my clothes, one piece at a time and wait for her to see what's plainly hidden in my tattoos and call me on it. She'll know for sure how I feel about her once she sees them. Although her gaze roams all over my body, it never seems to settle on any one spot.

Once I'm naked too, she lays herself down on my bed. I crawl to her, dropping kisses on her bare skin, all the way to her face.

"You're so beautiful," I tell her.

She smiles, leans up for a kiss.

I'll never get tired of her mouth. Kissing

her is my new favorite thing. But with every swipe of her tongue, my dick gets harder and harder.

I shift my body so I'm over hers. She spreads her thighs making room for me, but I keep my upper body braced off of her. I don't want her to panic if she starts to feel closed in.

Her knees come up on either side of my hips, effectively opening up her pussy. My dick slides between her slick folds. She's so hot and so wet.

"I don't want to hurt you," I say. I rock myself into the cradle of her thighs. Fuck, I'm not going to last. She's going to make me shoot off like a pubescent boy.

"Please," she begs. "I'm aching, Zane."

"I know, Starfish, I'm going to make it all better for you. But it might be a little uncomfortable when I first push in."

"You're not small," she says.

"No, I'm not. Do you want me to put on a condom, or are you on the pill? I'm clean and haven't been with anyone in a very long time."

Her head tilts on the mattress. "How long?"

"Years. It's been years, Emmy."

"I didn't realize you were celibate. I mean, not that it was any of my business."

I grin down at her. "So, condom?"

"Oh, no. I want the first time to be just us. I am on the pill though."

I notch myself at her entrance, so hot and slick, and press forward. I kiss her then, in hopes of distracting her from any pain. Our tongues glide against one another and I thrust forward in one hard push.

She winces and makes a noise in her throat. But I keep kissing her, letting her body grow accustomed to me.

I pull back to see how she's doing, and she looks up at me. "Does it bother you that I've never done this before?" she asks.

"What? Fuck no. I wish I hadn't." It's on my tongue to tell her that I wish I had saved myself for her. But it's foolish. I had already given it up before we even met. "I was an idiot for a while in my late teens."

She wiggles beneath me. "I think you can try moving now."

I pull back slowly, then push back in. Shallow at first, but she's so slick that moving inside her is a perfect slide despite her gripping me like a vice.

"I can feel your piercing," she says. "Oh." Her eyes widen. "Yeah, that's hitting right at that spot." Her breath hitches. "Does it feel good to you?"

"Starfish, you feel incredible. So good I'm trying to keep from coming too fast."

"You can do that whenever. I'm pretty sure it's statistically improbable that I'll climax during intercourse. Especially not the first time."

I laugh because I can't help myself. "You're adorable. But also, fuck statistics. I'm going to make you come on my dick."

She gives me a shy smile. "I'm not opposed."

Her ankles cross behind my back and her thick thighs hold me close to her body. I keep my rhythm true, making sure my piercing does drag across her G-spot. She grips my biceps as I thrust in and out of her.

I slip a hand in between us and find her clit. Small circles around the hood are all it takes for her to start moaning.

"Oh, oh, Zane. That feels really good."

"Yeah, it really fucking does. Christ, Emmaline, you're squeezing my dick so good."

She goes completely still beneath me, then her pussy convulses around my cock. She cries out and that's all it takes. I pump into her and come, and it's the single most amazing orgasm of my life. I growl her name as I ride out my climax.

I kiss her again, soft gentle sips at her lips. Then I withdraw and stand.

"Stay right there. I'll be back."

When I come back in, she's lying there all spread out on my bed like she's immobilized.

"You all right, Starfish?" I ask. Then I move the damp cloth I brought in over the tender spot between her legs.

"You have a most excellent bottom, Zane Miller," she says.

I laugh as I clean off her pussy.

"It's weird to think that we could have been doing that for years."

I laugh and crawl into bed next to her. "Do you want to take a shower or anything?"

She turns her head to face me and gives me a dreamy smile. "No. My body is sated and warm and kinda sleepy. I don't want to wake myself back up all the way."

"Can I hold you?" I ask.

"Yes. I think I might like that."

I roll onto my back and hold my arms out to her and she scoots closer. Her full curves press to my side and her head rests on my shoulder. I breathe in her hair and I want so badly to tell her that I'm in love with her. But I know instinctively she's not ready to hear those words.

Her legs shift. One covers mine, then moves off, then presses against me again. Her shoulders wiggle a little as she adjusts her head.

"What's the matter? It's okay if the cuddling is too much for you," I tell her.

"No, I think it's fine."

"But you're restless."

She leans up on her elbow. "It's just that I don't know what we're supposed to do now. What is the post-coital protocol? If we were characters in a book or movie, we'd either have a fight or have a big emotional conversation." She frowns. "None of that feels right for us. We don't have fights, and we already know everything about one another."

I chuckle. "There are no rules. We're not characters. We're real people. Real best friends. So, we do whatever the fuck we want to do."

"Okay, but what would you normally do after you've had sex with a hookup or whatever?"

My gut tightens at the thought of touching someone else. "I have zero interest in talking or thinking about another woman while I'm here with you. Besides, I told you, it has been years since my last hookup or whatever." I boop her nose.

It pulls a smile to her face. "Okay so we can do whatever we want?"

"Correct."

"Then let's watch *The 5th Element* again."

"Naked cuddling and my favorite movie. You just made my dreams come true, Starfish."

chapter
nine

Emmaline

I leave Zane's bed and house before he wakes up. Interesting that he sleeps like the dead. Since we've never had a sleepover before, I didn't know his sleeping habits. Like the fact that he's a snuggler but gave me room to choose when or if I wanted to be snuggled. Further proof that he knows me better than anyone.

I run home and get dressed, then head to the office. I don't normally go into the office on Mondays, but JD, my brother, texted yesterday and said he'd be in today. Normally JD works at the main office in Austin since his business partner, Hayes Crawford, moved back to Saddle Creek.

In any case, I want to see JD and show

him the work I've done on the current project because I think I have a solution to their problem.

I go into the breakroom first to get some hot tea. I didn't want to take the time or make the noise to do it at home since I didn't want to wake up Lily. She'd want to know all the details about last night and I'm not sure I'm ready to tell her.

"Hello, Emmaline," a voice says from behind me.

I turn and see Daniel. "Uh, hi."

"You look very nice in that outfit," he says, his voice is wooden, stilted, and just plain awkward.

Also, I'm wearing a version of what I always wear: yoga pants with a graphic tee. In other words, I'm not wearing anything special. He, too, is wearing his usual. Khakis and a tight-plaid button-down shirt. Well, the shirt itself isn't tight, but rather the print of the plaid. I'm pretty sure he has that shirt in every imaginable combination of colors.

I take my tea from the counter and turn to leave.

"Emmaline, wait. I wanted to ask you something," Daniel says.

I nod for him to continue.

"I was wondering if you might like to get

lunch sometime, or coffee or any other beverage?"

"Oh, that's very kind of you to ask, but I don't date coworkers." The lie falls from my lips as if it's the absolute truth. Though in many ways, it is the truth. I've never actually dated a coworker, and despite my initial thoughts, I have zero desire to date Daniel.

Sadly, the person I want to date is unavailable, at least outside of dating and sexual lessons. I'm not sure I can have any more of those without getting my heart completely torn to shreds. I have to figure out how to go back to where we were before. Before I knew what it felt like to kiss Zane. Touch him. Before I knew what it was like for him to put his hands and mouth all over me and make me feel like I've never felt before. Like, like my mind was silent and all I could feel was him and the pleasure he was pulling from my body. It was peaceful. But exhilarating.

"Oh," Daniel says, pulling me from my thoughts. "I get that. I just you know, we're—"

"Similar," I say.

He smiles. "Yes, we are."

"I learned recently that sometimes you need some differences, too, for compatibility. And, you know, one of those differences, I guess, needs to be that we work in different places."

He nods stiffly.

I smile and leave the break room and head to my brother's office. When I get there, I find JD behind the desk and Hayes, his business partner, and my prom date (long story),) sitting across from JD's desk.

"Oh, this is a room full of trouble," I say.

"Emmaline, I swear you get more and more gorgeous every time I see you," Hayes says. He stands and pulls me into a tight hug.

"Thank you. Congratulations on your marriage and upcoming baby." No one ever thought Hayes Crawford would move back to Saddle Creek, but evidently all it took was one night with Rory Reynolds and here he is.

Emmy," JD says, then gives me a hug too. "I'm glad you're here. I know you don't normally come in on Mondays, but I wanted you to be the first to know, aside from Hayes, because it was a decision he and I made together. But we are officially moving the headquarters of H&J Funds here to Saddle Creek. We'll keep the Austin office open as a satellite branch. But I am moving back home."

I squeal and hug my brother again. Because JD's always been the very best. Aside from Zane, he's the guy that knew that I didn't like crowds or loud noises or any number of other things. He took care of me. He protected me.

Hayes and JD have been best friends for years. They were already off in college by the time Lily and I were juniors in high school. Evidently, one day my brother was talking to Hayes about the fact that his two sisters didn't have dates to the prom because boys our age were "too stupid to see that different is awesome!" At least that's the story as I heard it.

So it was that Hayes—arguably the most attractive man in Saddle Creek (though my vote goes to Zane)—took me and my twin sister to the prom. And all of the girls were jealous.

We finish chatting and then I show them the work I've done.

Then the office door bursts open and in walks Zane, breathing heavily and looking rather harried.

I come to my feet. "Zane? What's the matter?"

"The matter is that I woke up alone in bed this morning. There was no sign of you. No note. No text."

My cheeks heat because he's saying all of this in front of my big brother.

"You don't even work in the office on Mondays," he snaps. Then he glances at my brother. "JD, Hayes," he says, nodding at each of them. "Sorry to intrude. I need to borrow Emmaline for a bit." Without waiting for a response, he picks me up, fireman style, and leaves the office.

I hear Hayes laughing as Zane makes his way to the elevator.

"Zane, I can walk."

"No talking yet, Starfish. We're gonna talk. Well, I'm gonna talk and you're gonna listen. But first we're getting out of here."

chapter
ten

Zane

I don't speak to her the entire drive to my house. Once we get there, I help her out of the car and hold her hand until we get inside. Then I press her against the door and kiss the hell out of her.

Now that I can kiss and touch her, I don't ever want to stop. Initially, she kisses me back, but then she pushes me away.

"What are you doing?" she asks. "You said you wanted to talk."

I nod. "I wanted to do that, too. I didn't like waking up without you in my bed."

"Well, you're going to have to get used to it. I don't want to have any more lessons," she says.

Her words slice into me. "Is that what

last night was for you? A lesson?" The question is torn from me and my words come out harsher than I mean them to, in a tone I've never used with her.

She flinches, taking another step back from me, her eyes wide and hurt. If I didn't know better, I'd think she was about to cry, which she never does. I take a step closer to her, but when I reach out a hand, she pulls back farther, wrapping her arms around herself. When she turns away from me, and it feels like she's fucking ripping my heart out.

"Shit. Emmy, I'm sorry."

Her back is to me and she peers over her shoulder at me. "You've never yelled at me."

"I didn't mean to yell." Fuck. I feel like I kicked a puppy, but she's right. I've never raised my voice with her.

I know I look like a brute of a guy. I yell at Ian all the time, because he's my brother and a grumpy asshole on top of that. Not a genuine asshole, just in the way that all older brothers are assholes. In school I used to get in fights all the time, because I was pissed off at the world. I work out all the damn time because I've basically been sexually frustrated since I met Emmy when I was seventeen. So, yeah, I look like a guy who would yell at a lot. But I don't. And I have never yelled at Emmy, because she hates loud noises and... fuck, because she's my girl. My starfish. So prickly and delicate and strange and beautiful all at the same time.

And I'm so fucking terrified that I've messed this up. That I pushed too hard, asked for too much from her, and ruined everything between us. Destroyed everything that's good and perfect in my life.

Now, all of a sudden, I'm the one who's crying.

Jesus, Ian would have a field day with this.

I'm not sobbing like a baby or anything, but there are definitely tears. And the threat of snot. Yeah, I'm a disaster.

I scrub a hand down my face, praying that she doesn't notice the tears and that I can find the words to fix this. I turn away and pace to the far side of the room, trying to get my emotions under control.

"Are you mad at me?" she asks in that same small voice.

I turn back to look at her. The length of the room separates us, but suddenly, it feels like miles.

"No, I'm not mad at you. I could never be mad at you. If anything, I'm mad at myself. Fuck, Emmy, I'm in love with you."

She shakes her head. "No, you're not.

You're just saying that because you're my best friend and you *have* to love me."

"Goddammit, woman, stop telling me what I do and don't feel. Remember last night's lesson?"

Her cheeks turn pink. She steps away from me and paces the length of my living room. "I have to think for a minute."

Okay, thinking is good. Thinking means she's not walking away yet.

"I'm not going anywhere, Starfish. You want some water?"

She shakes her head. "None of this makes any sense. We started this whole thing because of my misguided intention to date a coworker." Her eyes squeeze shut. "It made so much sense. Daniel and I being together. We're both incredibly intelligent, similarly different, both work with computers." She holds up a finger. "Neither of us are conventionally attractive. We make sense."

I blow out a breath, clenching and releasing my fists, because if I have to stand here and listen to her talk about how great fucking Daniel is, I might to excuse myself to go punch something. But that's not even the worst part of what she said.

"First of all, I'm going to correct you on something very crucial," I say.

She frowns. "Okay."

"You are fucking gorgeous. You are a beacon, shining so damn bright, I can't believe I get to look at you every day. So find commonality with Daniel if you must, but not there. Now continue."

She swallows visibly. "Do you know what happened today? I bet you can't even guess."

"Tell me."

"Daniel asked me out on a date."

My fists clench at my sides because this fucking guy... He's lucky I didn't know that when I saw him at the office this morning. I force myself to nod. "And?"

"I told him no!" She throws up her arms. "I can't imagine any other man touching me or kissing me but you."

I want to pump my fist in the air, because now we're getting somewhere. Finally. But she's still frowning.

"I do not see a problem with that."

"But we—you and me—screwed everything up."

I move and sit on the sofa. "Come sit with me and finish talking?" I pat my lap.

She stares at me for a minute, licks her lips and walks to me. But she sits next to me, not on my thighs.

"You and I don't fit, Zane. I mean we hardly make sense as friends. You're this wild sexy guy, and I'm—"

I grab her hand and still it. "But am I? Am I really so wild?"

She frowns, not meeting my gaze, like she's trying to pull up a memory. "You got in a lot of fights in high school. And you've always had a reputation for—" She cuts herself off, a blush rising in her cheeks.

Yeah. That. My reputation with women. I'm going to circle back to that.

Since she didn't sit on my lap, I move to sit on the coffee table, so that I'm right in front of her, my legs bracketing hers, because I need her to be looking at me.

"Do you remember the first time we met?"

She shrugs. "I think it was that time I got detention, my senior year."

I grin at her. "Yeah, it was. I was already in there because, fuck, I got detention all the time. But I was alone in there just sketching in my spiral notebook, and in you walk. Those pale blonde braids and your Hogwarts t-shirt. The whole room was empty except for me, and in that sea of unoccupied desks, you came and sat right next to me."

"You remember all of that?"

"I remember everything about that day." Our high school wasn't that big, so of course I'd seen her around school before, but we didn't exactly roll with the same crowd. She was in all the advanced classes, some of them so advanced she had to take them online for college credit. But I'd seen her around, drifting through the halls, apart from most everyone else, like she was encased in a glass dome. Lovely, untouchable, ethereal. So it shocked the hell out of me when she sat down next to me. "You turned and looked at me and said, 'What are you in for?' I thought it was the funniest thing."

"Well, I was annoyed that I got sent there and I wanted to know if you were there for the same reason."

"For reading a novel in my science class? No."

"I was done with all my work!" she shrieks. "I still think that detention was BS."

"You said as much that day. But then you started talking about starfish. You just busted out with all these random facts. 'Hey, did you know starfish can grow back their limbs? They also don't have any blood.'" I smile and shake my head. "You blew my mind that day. You never looked at me like the 'bad guy' in detention; you just started talking to me."

"You started calling me 'Starfish' right after that," she says wistfully, but then shakes her head. "I never understood that."

"Why I called you Starfish?"

"No. Why you just... befriended me.

People didn't do that to me back in high school. They didn't really talk to me much or want to be with me. And then all of a sudden you were just there in my life. This guy that everyone thought was the coolest guy in school and you wanted to spend time with me."

The way she says that—about people not wanting to hang with her—so matter-of-factly, like it was not a big deal and it didn't hurt her feelings, when I know it did. That nearly breaks my heart all over again. Because she's amazing. And I knew it the moment we met.

I've done a lot of stupid shit in my life, but even I was smart enough to see how special she was. I made plenty of mistakes getting from there to here. There were a couple of years when I pretty much fucked any woman I could, thinking I could fuck away my feelings for Emmy.

And let me tell you, I was lucky that I didn't screw up my whole life during that time. Lucky I didn't get some woman pregnant or catch anything. Lucky that my behavior didn't disgust Emmy and make her end our friendship. Thank God, it didn't take me long to realize I was being a dumbass and that no other woman in the world could replace her.

So, yeah, maybe I earned my reputation for being wild, but it's not who I am. Not anymore. Despite the tattoos and piercings.

"I'm not that wild," I say aloud. "Not anymore."

Not since I've pretty much devoted myself to her.

She gives a little eye roll. "But look at you."

"Okay, yeah, I've got piercings and tattoos." I stand briefly and tear off my shirt. "Yeah, let's talk about my tattoos." I drop my pants so I'm just standing before her in my boxers. I kick my discarded clothes away.

I hold out my left arm. "The week after I met you, as soon as I turned eighteen, I got my first tattoo. I marked that occasion, inked you into my skin because I knew the day I met you, my entire life changed." I point to the starfish. Originally it was there all alone, now it's blended into the coral reef I have on that sleeve.

She tips her head to the side, staring at that tattoo like she never even considered its significance.

Then I start pointing out all the others. The tattoo on my chest, runes for earth, air, fire, and water from *The 5th Element*, with the negative space between them forming a star shape. The tribal tattoo on my shoulder, with what looks like plumeria blossoms woven through it. But each blossom is actually a starfish.

Finally, I hold out my right arm, where the sleeve is a tribute to all the sci-fi shows we both love. There's a night sky populated by the Serenity, the Millennium Falcon, and the Galactica.

"Look at this one."

She glanced at my arm. "Yes, your sci-fi sleeve. I still think you need to add the Enterprise."

My lips twitch, because she's been giving me hell about that for years. "Yeah, yeah. I will. But look at the stars."

It's so subtle no one has ever even noticed. Only Ian knows and he laughed his ass off the whole time he did the tattoo—and since it's a night sky it took for-fucking-ever.

She leans closer, squinting. "Are the stars ..." She looks up at me. "Are each of those stars a starfish?"

"Yeah, I am literally covered in you."

I point to the newest one, the one I added to the coral reef. "This one I did last week when you asked me to teach you how to be in a relationship with another man."

She sucks in a breath. "Zane."

"So don't tell me that I'm not in love with you. Because you've been making me a better man and making my life so much more amazing than I anticipated."

"You offered to help because you're my best friend. And we slept together because I turned you on," she says.

She still hasn't caught up to me yet. I sit back on the sofa and lift her into my lap. "Yes. I'm your best friend. And yes, I love you like that." I squeeze her hips. "But the truth is, I'm your best friend, Emmy, *because* I'm in love with you."

She stares at my face.

"You told me so many times over the years that you were not a couple person. You'd never be in a romantic or physical relationship. So, I became your friend because I thought it was the only way I'd ever have you. I wasn't going to squander that opportunity for anything."

Her finger goes to the starfish on my chest, the one right over my heart. Then she leans in. "Are those my initials?" she asks, tracing the lines of the letters.

"Yeah. I thought for sure you'd notice yesterday when I took off my shirt."

"I was too distracted by your muscles and then by your dick," she says with a grin.

"Emmy, listen to me. If you need me to go in front of the whole damn town and do something dramatic to prove to you that I'm in this for good, I'll do it. You know I will."

She releases a watery laugh and I realize she's crying.

I swipe at the tears on her cheeks.

"Thanks for the offer, but I don't want you to do that. That sounds like it would be really loud and crowded."

I bark out a laugh and pull her to my chest. "Fuck, I love you."

"I love you too, Zane."

"I know you might not ever want the same things that I want. And that's okay. I don't want to pressure you, ever, to do something you're not comfortable with. But I'm never going anywhere. And there will never be another woman for me besides you."

"It might take me a while to figure out how to do all of this, but I trust you." Then she kisses me. It's not a wild and dirty kiss, but rather one that's sweet and soaked in contentment. Then she leans forward, snuggling into my chest and lays her head on my shoulder.

I would have waited my whole life for this woman's love, but just like she always does, she surprises me.

chapter
eleven

Zane

"I still don't understand why you have to do this. Your skin is perfect as it is. Flawless," I say.

"Oh for fuck's sake, calm down," Ian says. "She's fine. She's not even wincing."

"I want to do this," Emmy reminds me.

I take a step closer and she shakes her head.

"No. Stay over there. I don't want you to see it until it's done."

I rake my fingers through my hair and blow out a breath. But I stay where they told me to stand. Over in the corner of the room so I can't see any details. I stare at my brother sitting on his stool leaning over my love, tattoo gun in hand.

I bounce a bit on my feet because they don't want me to walk around, but I've got to do something with all this nervous energy.

Ian spins on his stool to glare at me. "Goddammit, Zane, at least pretend you're a fucking professional. You've inked thousands of tats. You've gotten hundreds yourself. What is the matter with you?"

"It's different when it's your girl. Someday you'll see."

My brother's jaw tightens. He's a sworn bachelor, but I think it's only a matter of time before he falls hard.

"Why don't you have a drink?" Ian suggests.

"Because I don't want a fucking drink."

"I'm good, Zane. I promise," Emmy assures me.

"I don't like my brother being that close to your tits, Starfish."

"I'm not looking at her tits," Ian growls. "She's like my fucking sister, you asshat." He wipes with his rag and then leans back. "Thankfully she only wanted something small and I'm done." Ian stands and grins down at Emmy. "Looks good. Really good."

"Can I see now?" I ask.

Ian goes to leave the room, but then he stops short. "Don't you dare fuck in here when I leave. I don't want to have to sterilize the room."

She holds her hand out to me and I go to her side. She has her other hand covering up the newly inked skin.

"You have me all over your body. I wanted one that represented you permanently in my skin. If I'm your starfish, then you're the ocean water that holds me and protects me and pumps through my veins instead of blood." Then she moves her hand.

There, right above her breasts is the water symbol from The 5th Element. It's an exact replica of the one on my own chest.

"Now when we hug, our tattoos will press together. I'm sure that's a little silly, but I liked the idea of it," she says.

I pull her to her feet. "It's not silly at all, it's fucking perfect. You're fucking perfect." I kiss her, careful not to touch her chest.

"No sex in there!" Ian yells again.

Emmy and I laugh and break apart. I finish the aftercare for her tattoo and she grabs my hand.

"Let's go back to my place and have sex. Lily is out of town."

"Oh, did she finally go to find that guy? Her pen pal or whatever?" I ask.

"Yes. I hope she doesn't get murdered. I

would know though, right? I mean the whole twin thing?"

"Yeah, Starfish, you would know."

epilogue

Emmaline

I'm working at the office today, and so normally I'd meet Zane at Ruthie's. But today I texted him and told him I was swamped with work, and could he bring lunch to me instead?

Of course he agreed, because he loves me. I'm not just talking about the emotion that he obviously feels, but he loves me in the verb sense of the word. His every action demonstrates how he cares about me and it's addictive.

He's taught me so much in the few months we've been an official couple. Some people in town said they thought we'd been a couple for years. All that time I couldn't envision it myself—wouldn't let myself, and half the dang town thought it was already true.

There's a knock on my office door and those delicious nerve bubbles swim through my tummy. He pokes his head in and grins at me.

"Hey Starfish, you working hard?"

"I am. But I'm starving. Come in."

He comes inside carrying to-go bags from Ruthie's, and I clear off a spot on my desk for him to set down the food.

I stand and walk around him, closing my door and locking it.

His brows raise. "What are you doing, Emmy?"

"I want you to be a bad boy," I say.

It's a game we play sometimes because the truth of the matter is, my love is the sweetest man in the world. He might look like a bad boy, but he has the most gentle heart, which is just what I need.

But sometimes, I ask him to be the bad boy so he'll use that filthy talk on me. And boss me around, but only in a sexy way.

"In here?" he asks.

"Yep. In here." I push him slightly so his body is backed up to my office door. Then I drop to my knees and unbutton his jeans. I tug down his zipper.

Those sapphire blue eyes of his darken as

he licks his lips. "You need my cock, Emmaline, is that what's going on here?"

I nod.

"Reach in there and pull it out, then," he says.

I do as he tells me and wrap my fingers around his rapidly hardening shaft.

"What do I do with it?" I ask, feigning innocence.

"Lick it."

I lean forward and lick him straight up to the tip.

"Fuck," he hisses. "Now tongue my piercing."

So I do that, sliding my tongue all around the small barbell.

"That's it. Look at you on your knees in front of me worshiping my dick. Fuck, Starfish, you are my perfect dream."

I slide my mouth down, sucking him inside. I keep moving my tongue and he grabs my head.

"Yeah, you know just how I like it, don't you? Goddammit, but you suck me good."

I reach up and cup his balls.

"Are you wet?" he asks.

I look up at him, still holding him in my mouth.

"Answer me. Is your pussy wet?"

I nod slightly, not wanting to stop what

I'm doing. But he grabs my chin and gently pulls me off.

"As good as your mouth feels, if my love is wet, she needs this dick inside her pussy." He helps me to my feet, then reaches for the hemline of my skirt. "Did you wear this today because you wanted me to come here and fuck you in your office?"

"Yes."

"Then you need to bend yourself over the desk."

I do just as he says, bracing my arms on the desk and bending my body in half. His fingers tickle the backs of my knees as he lifts my skirt. He pulls down my panties.

"Open your legs more," he says. Then I feel the fat head of his dick pressing against my entrance. I push back into him.

He thrusts inside me and I put a fist to my mouth to keep from crying out, but it's so good. He always feels so, so good.

"That's it, oh yeah, you're dripping on my dick you're so wet. Fuck, Emmy," he growls.

Then the only sounds in my office are our breathing, the slap, slap of our skin and the wet noises coming from my core.

"I love to watch your pussy take my cock. We were made for this. Your body was made just for mine. Your heart was made just for my heart. Goddammit, I love you so much."

He continues to thrust inside me and I'm so close.

"Say you'll be my wife, Starfish. Put me out of my misery and marry me. Take me forever so I can take you forever."

And that's all it takes to tip me over the edge. I come with a groan, biting into my fist so I'm not too loud. He's right behind me, grunting quietly as he releases inside me.

When he pulls out, he grabs napkins from our take-out and cleans me up, then pulls my panties back into place.

I turn to face him. "Were you serious?"

"When I proposed?"

"Yes."

"I was. I intended to ask you with your slice of pie. I wasn't going to put the ring in the pie because I figured that would gross you out." He reaches into his pocket and pulls something out, holding it up for me.

It's a simple gold band with a flush mount solitaire. "So it won't snag on things," I say with a watery laugh.

"I know you."

"You do. And yes, of course I'll marry you. I'd like nothing better than to become your wife."

He picks me up and kisses me.

My stomach growls.

He sets me down, slides the ring on my finger and pulls me to sit in his lap. "Let's get you fed."

"You take such good care of me," I say.

"Always and forever."

2nd epilogue

From the *Saddle Peek*

RUMORS ARE FLYING ALL *over our illustrious little town that a certain "Bad Boy of Country Music" will be returning to his roots. I'm sure we all remember what happened the last time Micah Stone was in town...*

I hope you loved Zane and Emmy's story. Please consider **leaving me a review**. Ian is getting his own book! Find his story in **Hot Mess Wedding**. Want to know what happens with Emmy's twin when she goes off to find her grumpy pen-pal in **Lily's Forest**.

Keep scrolling for an excerpt of Harper's book, **Lone Star Best Friend**.

Want more "Bad Boys of Saddle Creek"? **Micah** is coming in March.

thank you for reading!

Join my newsletter for bonus epilogues, deleted scenes and a FREE BOOK.

If you liked this friends-to-lovers book, you'll enjoy these other *friendly* titles!

**Real Men Love Curves
I Kissed a Ghoul
Knocking Up His Best Friend
Rules of the Friend Zone**

See ALL of my books.

*Want to connect with me?
Join my Facebook VIP reader
group: Baxter Babes
Friend me on Facebook
Follow me on Pinterest
Follow me on Instagram*

Follow me on [Twitter](#)
Follow me on [Bookbub](#)
Follow me on [Goodreads](#)
Visit my [website](#) for excerpts of all my books.
Visit my [author page on Amazon](#) for links to all of my books.

I also love to hear from readers so feel free to [drop me a line](#) anytime.

excerpt from lone star best friend

HARPER

I stare at the words on my phone until they blur, the tears gathering in my eyes making them impossible to see. But it doesn't matter, I've already committed them to memory.

> Rory Reynolds is expecting! The owner of the small hobby farm and traveling petting zoo has been knocked up by one of the two remaining Crawford brothers. But just who is the father-to-be? Did Rory catch the eye of the elusive playboy, Hayes, or the heart of the youngest, Johnny?

I have no one to be angry with but myself. I'm twenty-two years old and I've spent the better part of the last eight years being stupidly in love with my best friend, Johnny Crawford. That's on me. I should have known better. I mean we barely made sense as friends let alone as a couple, still my stupid heart wanted what it wanted.

Is it a pathetic cliché that what my chubby, dorky heart wants is his handsome blond face? Yes. Yes it is.

In my defense (and in defense of my

stupid dorky heart), I don't just want his handsome face and hot body. Johnny is so much more than just a hot guy.

He's a good guy. The best guy.

At least, that's what I've been telling myself all along.

Maybe it's foolish to be secretly in love with your best friend, but when your best friend is as great as Johnny is, how could I help it?

Except, now I'm questioning everything. Doubting everything.

Maybe this means that Johnny isn't the great guy I think he is.

Maybe I've been deluding myself all these years and he's a jerk who sleeps with women he barely knows.

That would suck.

You know what would suck even more?

If Johnny is the great guy I think he is.

Because if I know him as well as I think I do, then he's going to do the right thing. He's going to step up. He's going to marry her and make lots of stupidly beautiful babies with her.

Either way, my heart gets broken, I get left behind. Like fucking always.

Like the super mature woman I am, I scream into my pillow, then kick my heels into my mattress. A little tantrum never hurt anyone. But now I need to be done. Also, I need to get my chubby ass out of town, especially before Johnny gets into town.

Because I know he's coming. He's recently graduated from college and is moving back to Saddle Creek from Austin with his shiny degree. I need to figure things out before I see him again. It is time for me to get over Johnny once and for all.

It takes me only fifteen minutes to grab some stuff, then toss it in my old compact car. I turn on my angry playlist—which I've been listening to a lot lately—and head out of town.

My parents will be pissed, but this is the first and only time I've ever bailed on them. And I happen to know that Olive Herrington is coming into town and since she lived with my family for a year and worked at our ice cream shop during that time, she can help out while I'm gone. I hate leaving her since technically she's coming to see me. But I also am not a complete fool and I know that she's been in love with my older brother, Baker, for years.

He's been "moving home soon" for a while now. Ever since an injury ended his professional baseball career. But I'm pretty sure I know how to get him into town quickly. So I press the call button.

"Hey big brother," I say, careful to keep my tone even so he doesn't hear my sadness. Thankfully, Baker is not the kind of guy who is super in touch with his own emotions, let alone anyone else's. So if there are traces of my emotional despair lingering in my voice, he misses them. "You said to call if I ever needed you. I need you."

"What's going on?" he asks, his tone gruff.

The scrubby juniper trees and stunted oaks pass by out my window as I drive north towards Inks Lake, where our parents own a cabin. Inks is one of a chain of lakes that trail across central Texas. Inks is far enough from Austin and San Antonio that it's still mostly cottages, locals, and a sprawling state park. It's the perfect place to get lost for a few days. Or longer if I need it. "This weekend is PeachFest," I say.

"And?" he asks.

PeachFest is the biggest tourist weekend of the year, aside from the Bluebonnet Festival. Listen, small towns in Texas love their festivals. Since our family's ice cream shop, Sprinkles, sits in the center of town, this weekend generates a lot of business.

I take a deep, cleansing breath. "Mom's gonna freak out, but I've left town." I don't give Baker any time to ask me questions or make comments, I just barrel forward. "I know you're wondering what the hell I'm thinking leaving the shop on such a busy weekend and frankly, I'm not ready to talk about it yet."

"Are you in danger?"

"No. I'm safe."

"What do you need?" he asks.

"I know it's a lot to ask, but can you go home and work the shop? Also, you can be there to greet Olive when she gets in town. I feel terrible for leaving before she arrives, but I had to get out of town."

I barely hear the audible suck in of a breath Baker does.

"Did you say Olive is going to be there?"

"Yes." I bite down on my lip. This was definitely the right call to make.

"Olive?" he asks. "From England?"

"Do we know another Olive?"

"No. At least I don't. Olive is coming back to Texas?"

I roll my eyes. "Oh my God, did you get hit on the head? Pay attention, Bake. Yes, Olive is coming back. Can you go home to help at the shop? Please?"

"Yes, of course. I'll leave tonight."

We disconnect after a few more random exchanges where I still give him nothing.

I pull up to my family's lake cabin—

which is not luxurious in any sense of the word. It's literally just a small cabin my dad used to use when he fished and hunted more. Inks is a constant level lake, so the house is thirty feet from the water and surrounded by a grove of towering pecans. It's a classic log cabin with a single bathroom, a kitchen that's open to the living room, and a bedroom loft. Mom keeps threatening to add on a "proper bedroom" claiming she's too old to go up and down the ladder, but so far she hasn't made good on her threats. Which means the cabin is exactly as it's been all my life, cozy, welcoming, and steeped in nostalgia.

I get my bags inside in one trip as I didn't bring much. Just comfy clothes—soft cotton and elastic only—and food. Thankfully, I know everything is freshly cleaned because my parents were here recently. The minute I sit on the old sofa, my tears return with a vengeance.

I let myself cry, like an idiot for a while and then I wipe my face and video call Olive. I mean she's expecting to see me at my house and I'm just not there. Of course Olive is supportive and thankfully doesn't pry. Maybe she's just too British to press me for more details.

The one good thing about crying my eyes out most of the day is, I'm damned exhausted. So falling asleep happens without too much of an effort.

Unfortunately when I wake up, my eyes feel like I slept in a sand pit. I grab my phone to check the time, then stare at the red bubble indicating I have unread text messages. I click to open the window and see that I have several from Johnny and two from Zane.

I click on Zane's first because I know that no matter what, his won't make me sad or anxious or angry or anything like that.

> ZANE: If you want to start shadowing me, you can do it next week. Have you talked to your parents about time off?

> ZANE: btw, I'm gonna start the new season of that Marvel spin-off tonight if you wanna come by.

Zane. I smile, but it's bittersweet. I've known Zane almost as long as I've known Johnny, but we weren't friends until recently. Why couldn't I like Zane? He's really hot. In a way different way than Johnny is, but still ridiculously attractive.

I'm pretty sure that Zane is attracted to me, maybe even has a crush on me which is shocking considering how far apart we are on the hot meter. It's not that I think I'm unattractive. I know I have a pretty face. I've been told that my entire life.

You have such a pretty face.

But therein lies the problem, doesn't it?

Other girls get told they're pretty. Period. Not that only one aspect of them is attractive. My compliments were restricted to my face because my body was beyond society's standards of what constitutes beauty. But you know what? When you grow up literally in an ice cream parlor, you tend to eat it on the regular.

So yeah, I have a big booty and thick thighs that rub together when I walk. I have tummy rolls and my boobs are enormous, so much so that I haven't worn a swimsuit in this town since I was like nine. I'm not even kidding. I'm pretty sure no one even knows I know how to swim.

I hide my giant tatas beneath oversized sweatshirts or hoodies and pretend I'm cold all the time. It helps that I often am, at least when I'm at work. That's the one good thing about working for my parents.

And when I say "the one good thing" I mean it.

There are a lot of negatives to working for your parents. Topping the list is that, even though I'm twenty-two and a proper adult, they still treat me like a child. I can't grow up in their eyes, because I'm still the girl who started scooping ice cream at fourteen.

Which brings me to the second shitty thing about working at Sprinkles: I've been doing it since I was fourteen. Longer, if you consider how much time I spent there "just helping out."

My parents love Sprinkles. It's their dream and their passion. But it's never been mine. Yeah, I like ice cream. Who doesn't?

But it's not exactly the most intellectually stimulating work. I want more from life than scooping ice cream and making polite conversation with customers.

I want something creative and fulfilling and ... Just more.

Which is where Zane comes in. Zane co-owns The Needle Bards with his older brother. I've always been a doodler, sketching random things here and there on margins of school notes, napkins at Sprinkles and anything else I could get my hands on. When Zane had seen some of my sketches, he'd tossed out a random comment that at the time he probably hadn't even meant, something to the effect of, 'those would make cool ink.' And with those words it was like a gear or a notice or whatever clicked into place.

From then on, I would pepper him with questions about training and techniques and everything in between. I'd been toying with the idea of quitting Sprinkles and becoming an ink slinger ever since. Probably ridiculous since I don't even have a single tattoo myself. I'm going to get one eventually. Just haven't figure out yet the right design.

But if I go to work for Zane—assuming an apprenticeship with him isn't a colossal disaster—then then I won't be able to wear that kind of thing. Tattooing is such detailed work. I can't afford to get the cord tangled up in my sleeves or whatever. Not to mention I don't want to be sweating like a cow while I'm inking someone.

What am I even saying? I'm not going to quit my family's ice cream shop to become a tattoo artist.

Someone bangs on the cabin door and I nearly come out of my skin. Holy hell.

"Harper! Are you in there?"

Johnny. Shit!

"Harpsichord!" Knock, knock, knock.

I roll my eyes and go to the door because I know he's not going to go away. I swing it open.

"What are you doing here?" I ask.

He gives me that soft smile that makes my heart go all gooey, but right now I'm so damn mad at him I could spit. "Hey, Harps, whatcha doing at your daddy's fishing cabin? It's PeachFest weekend? Are you sick?" He shoulders his way into the cabin, with his big, stupid, broad shoulders that look entirely too good in that faded grey t-shirt.

He cups my face with those stupid big hands of his. All the Crawford men are tall, so it stands to reason that he's no different and he crouches a little to look into my eyes. His gaze searches my face, taking in every sign of grief, his expression of concern deepening with every second.

That gaze of his lays me bare and I'm terrified that he sees everything I've tried so long to hide from him. All the love, all the yearning, all the pent-up desire and sexual frustration. All the stupid pointless fantasies I've harbored.

"Sweetheart, you've been crying. Who made you sad? Did someone put their hands on you?" he asks.

Well, there's the most ironic question of the decade. I pull away from him.

"No, I'm fine."

"Harper Michelle Rhodes, do not lie to me. I am your best friend and I know you better than that," he says, his tone gruff and demanding. "Tell me what's wrong?"

What's wrong? What isn't wrong would be a better question. A shorter answer at least.

What's wrong is that I've spent too much of my life waiting. Too much time planning and not doing. I was so sure the future I had planned for myself—a future with Johnny—would someday be mine, I never came up with a backup plan. Johnny was plan A, B, and C. Johnny was my everything. Now that he's my nothing, I have nothing left.

I don't blame him. I blame myself, but he's an easier target to vent my anger on.

"I just needed some time away," I say, spinning away to face the other side of the room.

"During the busiest time of year for your parents' shop?"

I turn on him. "Is that what this is? Did my mother call you and send you to find me?"

He swallows and his Adam's apple bobs, drawing my attention to the scruff covering his jaw and throat. What's up with that?

Johnny is always clean shaven. Always.

But not today. Today he looks like he rolled out of bed after a bender and stumbled straight to his car.

I shake my head to clear away the image of Johnny in bed.

Get a grip! Do not think about that sexy jaw scruff. Do not notice how nice and thick his neck is or how it leads into those muscular shoulders.

"No, no one sent me. I got home yesterday ready to see you, only to be told that you were missing, and no one knew where you were."

He threads his fingers through his hair and again I notice how uncharacteristically messy it looks. Johnny's not one of those guys who spends time fixing his hair per se, but he's generally a tidy guy. His blond locks definitely look like he's done this exact movement more than once.

Then I realize he's got dark smudges under his eyes. Eyes that are normally crystalline green, but today are shot through with red veins of exhaustion. I frown.

"Why do you look like shit?" I ask.

"Nice of you to notice. Because, genius, I've been up all night trying to find you. I about lost my mind when I heard you were missing. Christ, Harps, I didn't know if you were hurt and bleeding on the side of the road somewhere or what."

My heart thumps wildly and a stab of guilt shoots through me. "That's dumb."

His jaw clenches and his green eyes narrow.

Johnny and I have been friends long enough that of course we've had our share of disagreements and fights. But I've never seen him look legitimately angry with me.

I lift my brows. "Wow, Johnny, you look mad enough to punch me."

"Spank you, maybe, never punch." He grabs my biceps and pushes me backwards until I fall over onto the sofa. "Now talk. What the hell is wrong with you?"

Spank me? Heat flushes through me at the mental image of me bent over his knee, my ass bare to his hand.

Why is that so damn hot? And why am I getting all aroused when he's making demands like a bossy asshole?

"Maybe I'm tired of people making decisions for me," I shoot back. "I'm tired of people telling me what to do. I'm tired of everybody thinking they know everything about me."

"What the hell does that mean?"

"It means I'm tired of spending my life trying to be the person everyone thinks I am instead of person I want to be."

He just looks at me like I'm speaking another language. "Okay. Fine. But why are you mad at me about this. I haven't even been in town."

I release a noise in the back of my throat because he's been in town enough. Obviously since he knocked Rory up.

"You know what? I actually don't have to talk to you when I'm upset. It's part of being an adult and leaving town. I wanted to be alone because I didn't want to talk to anyone."

I stand up and start going through the motions of getting ready. After all, if I'm going to be this new version of myself, the first step is to take Zane up on his offer. True, I haven't confirmed a set time to meet Zane, but if I pretend I have somewhere to be, Johnny will be forced to leave.

I step into the tiny bathroom and brush my teeth, doing my best to ignore Johnny's presence in the house. Which is damn near impossible because I'm just naturally attuned to him. Also, he's just a big guy. Then I quickly change clothes, only to realize that the door hadn't shut all the way and Johnny's hot glare is staring at me in the reflection of the old mirror.

Well, whatever. It's not like he's gonna take one look at my bra-enclosed boobs and pledge his undying devotion to me. I throw my hair up in a messy bun, then slip on my shoes.

"Sorry you came all this way." I try for emotional restraint, but probably still sound pissy and annoyed. "Thanks for checking on me; I'm fine. I'm not dead or anything. Now I have to go to work."

"Now?" he barks.

"Yes. Exactly." Was I going back to Saddle Creek to go to Sprinkles? No, no, I was not. I was going to Zane's shop and I was going to do something different with my life.

My parents might be disappointed when they realize I'm quitting Sprinkles for good, but they'll understand eventually. They've always been nauseatingly supportive.

It's time for me to live my life on my own terms. Even if that means walking away from the life I thought I was destined to live.

Buy **Lone Star Best Friend** or read for FREE in KU!

about the author

USA TODAY BESTSELLING AUTHOR, Kat Baxter writes fast-paced, sweet & STEAMY romantic comedies. Readers have dubbed her "The Queen of Adorkable." and her books "laugh-out-loud funny," and "hot enough to melt your kindle." She lives in Texas with her family and a menagerie of animals. Kat is the pseudonym for a bestselling historical romance author.

What readers have said about Kat's books:

"Kat Baxter is my catnip!" ~ Goodreads review

"Whenever I need my sexy nerdy dirty talking romance fix, I know Kat Baxter has my back!" ~Goodreads review

"How does Kat Baxter make me fall in love with her characters in just 12 short chapters? It's coz she's a freaken magic weaver with her words!!" ~ Amazon review

"You'll instantly fall in love." ~Goodreads review

"Swoon. I could not get enough of this story and fell in love with both these characters!" ~Amazon review

"... the chemistry between them is instant and off the charts!" ~Amazon review

"... original, hot, and a hoot!" ~Amazon review

"DAMN it's hot." ~Amazon review

"... sweetness, heat and humor. By the time the story was over, my cheeks hurt from smiling so hard." ~Amazon review

Made in the USA
Columbia, SC
14 July 2024